Cathedral Music Press Presents

W9-CVO-127

Sacred Solos

for the

Flute

Vol. 1

Works by: *Bach, Corelli, Pachelbel, Massenet, Handel, Schubert*

with Piano & Organ Accompaniments

Compiled & Arranged by

Dona
Gilliam

Mizzy
McCaskill

The cover is a photo-reproduction of a hand-marbled original. Only a few artists in the U.S. are currently involved in the creation of marbled papers.

©*Marbled Papers by Susan Browning Pogany, 520 Louisiana, Lawrence, KS 66044*

Cathedral
MUSIC PRESS

1 2 3 4 5 6 7 8 9 0

Visit us on the Web at www.melbay.com — E-mail us at email@melbay.com

CONTENTS

Sacred Solos for the Flute Volume I-CD
Piano: Mizzy McCaskill & Dona Gilliam
Organ: Gretchen Franz
(Mount Lebanon United Methodist Church, Pittsburgh, PA)

This CD contains both organ and piano accompaniment tracks for all pieces in Mel Bay's *Sacred Solos for the Flute Volume I*. All pieces in which the flute begins on a pick-up note or downbeat are given an added introduction that is not found in the score. This added introduction establishes the tempo and allows the soloist to enter with the recorded accompaniment at the appropriate time.

1. Introduction (:37)

2. Tuning Note (A) (:26)

3. ORGAN: *Air* from the *Messiah*-George Frideric Handel (4:07)

4. PIANO: *Air* from the *Messiah*-George Frideric Handel (4:11)

5. ORGAN: *Ave Maria* Franz Schubert (3:45)

6. PIANO: *Ave Maria* Franz Schubert (3:45)

7. ORGAN: *Chorale* from *Cantata No. 147, Herz und Mund und Tat und Leben* Johann Sebastian Bach (3:27)

8. PIANO: *Chorale* from *Cantata No. 147, Herz und Mund und Tat und Leben* Johann Sebastian Bach (3:25)

9. ORGAN: *Sheep May Safely Graze* from *Cantata No. 208, Was mir behagt, ist nur die muntre Jagd*-Johann Sebastian Bach (4:03)

10. PIANO: *Sheep May Safely Graze* from *Cantata No. 208, Was mir behagt, ist nur die muntre Jagd*-Johann Sebastian Bach (3:54)

11. ORGAN: *Air* from *Overture in D*-Johann Sebastian Bach (3:03)

12. PIANO: *Air* from *Overture in D*-Johann Sebastian Bach (2:55)

13. ORGAN: *Sinfonia* from *Cantata No. 156, Ich steh mit einem Fuss im Grabe* Johann Sebastian Bach (4:40)

14. PIANO: *Sinfonia* from *Cantata No. 156, Ich steh mit einem Fuss im Grabe* Johann Sebastian Bach (4:34)

15. ORGAN: *Canon* Johann Pachelbel (2:37)

16. PIANO: *Canon* Johann Pachelbel (2:38)

17. ORGAN: *Meditation* from *Thaïs* Jules Massenet (3:51)

18. PIANO: *Meditation* from *Thaïs* Jules Massenet (3:44)

19. ORGAN: *Saraband* from *Sonata No. 8, Op. 5*-Arcangelo Corelli (1:53)

20. PIANO: *Saraband* from *Sonata No. 8, Op. 5*-Arcangelo Corelli (1:53)

AIR FROM THE MESSIAH
HE SHALL FEED HIS FLOCK

He shall feed His flock like a shepherd; and He shall gather the lambs with his arm, and carry them to His bosom, and gently lead those that are with young. (Isaiah XL, 11)

Come unto Him, all ye that labour, and are heavy laden, and He will give you rest. Take His yoke upon you, and learn of Him, for He is meek and lowly of heart, and ye shall find rest unto your souls. (Matthew XI, 28-29)

ORGAN
Sw. Flutes 8' + 4'
Ped. Bourdon 16', 8'

George Frideric Handel
(1685-1759)

Piano and Organ Accompaniment

AVE MARIA

Piano Accompaniment

Franz Schubert
(1797-1828)

AVE MARIA

ORGAN
L.H. Sw. Strings
R.H. Ch. Flute 8', Sw. to Ch.
Ped. Bourdon 16', Sw. to Ch.

Organ Accompaniment

Franz Schubert
(1797-1828)

CHORALE FROM CANTATA NO. 147
"HERZ UND MUND UND TAT UND LEBEN"

ORGAN

Sw.   Flute 8' + 4' + 2'
Gt.   Flute 8'
Ped. Bourdon 16', Flute 8'

Piano and Organ Accompaniment

Johann Sebastian Bach
(1685-1750)

17

21

SHEEP MAY SAFELY GRAZE
FROM CANTATA NO. 208

"WAS MIR BEHAGT, IST NUR DIE MUNTRE JAGD"

ORGAN

Sw. Flute 8' + 4'
Opt. Ped. Bourdon 16'

Piano and Organ Accompaniment

Johann Sebastian Bach
(1685-1750)

D.C. al Fine

D.C. al Fine

25

AIR FROM OVERTURE IN D

ORGAN
Sw. Flute 8'

Piano and Organ Accompaniment

Johann Sebastian Bach
(1685-1750)

26

SINFONIA FROM CANTATA NO. 156
"ICH STEH MIT EINEM FUSS IM GRABE"

ORGAN
Sw. Flute 8' + 4'

Johann Sebastian Bach
(1685-1750)

Piano and Organ Accompaniment

31

CANON

ORGAN
Sw. Flutes 8' + 4'
Gt. Flute 8'
Ped. Bourdon 16',
Sw. to Ped.

Piano and Organ Accompaniment

Johann Pachelbel
(1653-1706)

MEDITATION FROM THAÏS

Piano Accompaniment

Jules Massenet
(1842-1912)

37

MEDITATION FROM THAÏS

ORGAN

L.H. Sw. Strings
R.H. Ch. Flute 8', Sw. to Ch.
Ped. Bourdon 16', Sw. to Ch.

Organ Accompaniment

Jules Massenet
(1842-1912)

44

SARABAND FROM SONATA NO.8, OP.5

ORGAN
Sw. Flute 8'
Ped. Bourdon 16',
Sw. to Ped.

Arcangelo Corelli
(1653-1713)

Piano and Organ Accompaniment